FRIDAY'S TAIL TALE

by Eliza Elliot
based on the book by Lois Duncan
screenplay by Jeff Lowell and Bob Schooley & Mark McCorkle
Ready-to-Read

Simon Spotlight
New York   London   Toronto   Sydney

Based on the movie *Hotel For Dogs*™

SIMON SPOTLIGHT
An imprint of Simon & Schuster Children's Publishing Division
1230 Avenue of the Americas, New York, New York 10020
™Paramount Pictures. © 2008 DreamWorks LLC. All Rights Reserved.
All rights reserved, including the right of reproduction in whole or in part in any form.
READY-TO-READ, SIMON SPOTLIGHT, and colophon are registered trademarks of
Simon & Schuster, Inc.
Manufactured in the United States of America
First Edition
2 4 6 8 10 9 7 5 3 1
ISBN-13: 978-1-4169-7514-4
ISBN-10: 1-4169-7514-4

Who says a dog's life is easy?
Let me tell you, my life has
been no walk in the park!
I mean, just a few weeks ago
I was roaming the streets
looking for my next meal.
Mmmm . . . I remember that one . . .
lots of yummy MEAT!

Afterward all I wanted was a
nice, long scratch—but nope!
I can't speak human, but when
my buddies Andi and Bruce told me
to "go," I knew I had to scoot!
Something smelled funny too.
Either my buddies were scared,
or someone needed a bath!

So I waited for my buddies
back near their den. They always
made me wait by the window
before letting me inside. Strange!
Sometimes it was not that bad.
Bruce let me sleep with him.
I even had my own fluffy mat!

Their den was fine for sleeping, but their keeper was the worst cook ever! So I had to keep searching the streets for food. One day this human in a uniform looked at me really funny. I knew I had to scoot again! What is it with humans in uniforms?

Anyway, he caught up with me and picked me up! I had no idea where he was taking me!

Thank goodness my pals saved me!
They are so loyal! But just when
I thought we were safe, we were
on the run—again! But I knew
where we would be safe for sure.
I led and they followed me!

When we got there I could smell
that we were not alone. We had
company, but they were just dogs
like me! One was big and sturdy;
the other was small and fast.

I gave them a quick sniff and
realized they were friendly!
Then we went upstairs to play!
There was a huge bed up there.
I was wiped out, so I took a nice,
long nap with my new friends.

In the next few days my buddy
Bruce kept running from room
to room looking for stuff.
It seemed like a fun game, so
I joined in!

Then he started putting things
together and they moved!
Suddenly there were machines everywhere!
There was one that cleaned me—
and it knew all the right spots,
especially my belly!

The big dog liked the gadget
that put pictures on the wall.
And I could rest my paws while
my little friend fetched balls
again and again . . . and again!
I was just happy they both
finally stopped barking!

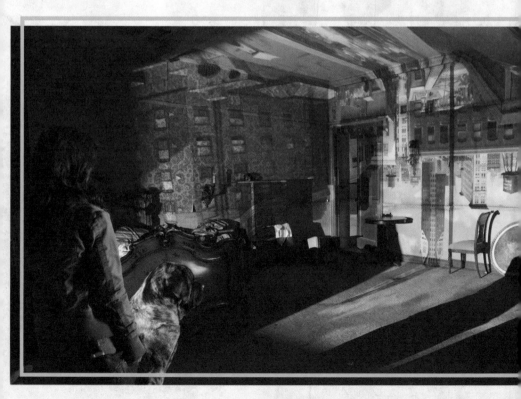

All of a sudden there were
so many dogs, it was like a play day
in the park that never ended!
Some of the new dogs were dirty,
stinky, and full of fleas—yuck!
Luckily one of the
keepers gave great baths.

Our days were full of things to do! Some dogs liked to hang their heads out of this opening and let the air blow on them. If I got too close I got covered in yucky slobber!

When we wanted to run around
there were all these fluffy
things we could chase.
Sometimes it was hard to tell
who was chasing who.
There were a couple of times
I almost got squished!

Watching the boxes was way more my speed. Sometimes a dog just needs to relax, you know?

My favorite time of day was always dinnertime! One of the machines served us yummy chicken bits.

Then I would always go to the room with the machine that made my smelly poop disappear! Finally I did not have to worry about stepping in it anymore. Boy, that used to really get my paws in a twitch.

One day I was sniffing around
and I found my buddy Andi
on the roof. She looked really sad.
I wanted to cheer her up,
but first I needed a snack! Then
I realized she was probably sad
because she needed one too!
I knew I could help!

A few days later I heard a loud noise in the kitchen. The dogs had gone totally wild! They were galloping through the halls, crashing through doors, and popping up all over the place! And they all seemed to be barking at me!

When my buddies finally came back
from wherever they had gone,
I smelled a weird scent on them.
If I had not known any better,
I would have thought they
were scared. But I knew better!

I guess I was wrong, though.
Suddenly all my friends were
snarling, and I realized the smell
was from that guy in the uniform!
Somehow he had found me!
Before I knew it we were all
running really fast!

Before I could bark I was back
with that uniformed guy, going
who-knows-where! But this time
I knew exactly what to do . . . I just
did my little collar trick and
I was free!

Then I found my buddies, and we
got everyone else home safe too!
It was a bit scary, but my buddies
had never let me down before.
I knew they would save us.

Finally we were home again!
But all these people followed us.
There were lots of uniforms.
I had had such a rough day and
I just wanted to sleep already!
Then this guy made everyone
quiet down. He must have been
the leader of the pack.

I did not know what he said,
but whatever it was,
he really turned the place around!
Sniff, sniff. Let me tell you—
everything smells a whole lot
better now!

The big guy and the little guy
are both top dogs here now,
just like me!

And there are even more machines
for us to play with! We do not even
have to climb the stairs on our own!

It is still sad when I have to say good-bye to my friends. But I can get behind it when I know they are leaving with great-smelling people!

So the first part of my life was pretty rough. But now things are great! There are people and dogs everywhere—and only good uniforms. But I still love being with my two favorite people most of all!

Well, there are my favorite buddies,
so it is time for me to go!
Sniff, sniff. Smells yummy!
I wonder what is for dinner?
Woof! Woof!